Disney FROZEN

An Amazing Snowman

Nina

To Mary, who knew what it meant to be
a friend and taught me well. I miss you.

—B.J.H.

To my husband, Eddy—thank you for all your
support and always trying to make me laugh.

—O.T.M.

ISBN 978-0-545-80688-6

Published by Scholastic Inc., 557 Broadway, New York, NY 10012,
by arrangement with Disney Press, an imprint of Disney Book Group.

12 11 10 9 8 7 6 5 4 3 2 1 14 15 16 17 18 19/0

Printed in the U.S.A. 40

First Scholastic printing, December 2014

Designed by Tony Fejeran

Disney

FROZEN

An Amazing Snowman

by Barbara Jean Hicks

illustrated by Olga T. Mosqueda

SCHOLASTIC INC.

Olaf is not
your everyday
snowman.

He
walks.

He
talks.

He even sings.

But those aren't the only things that make him special!

Olaf is special
because

he sees the
best in
everyone.

His brother,
Marshmallow,
is a playful
fellow . . .

Sven the reindeer
is forever trying to
kiss his nose . . .

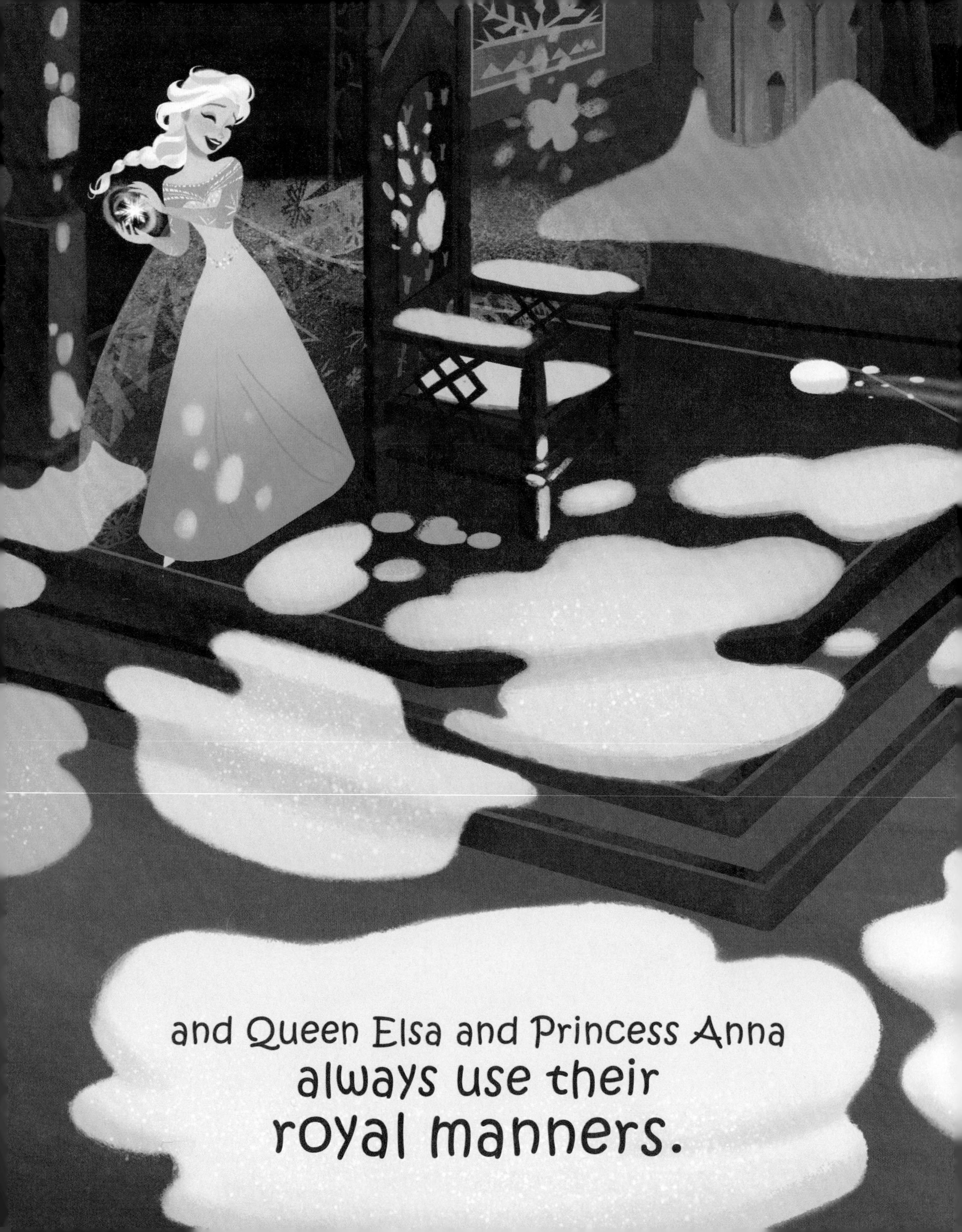

and Queen Elsa and Princess Anna
always use their
royal manners.

Olaf is special
because

he finds
beauty in
every day . . .

and because he dreams.

Olaf dreams about sand castles . . .

and ships sailing to new horizons . . .

and swimming with friendly sea creatures.

"Hi there!"

Olaf dreams about soaring in the sky . . .

and picking fresh fruit . . .

. . . and meeting new friends.
"That tickles!"

Olaf is special because in his eyes,

or winter,

every day is an adventure . . .

and
every
night
shines.

Olaf is
special because
he knows
that every
ending . . .

is a chance for a new beginning . . .

and
a
chance . . .

for a
nice, warm
hug!

The End.